The Wicked are not Allowed in the Garden

Eady H

Published by Eady H, 2024.

This is a work of fiction. Similarities to real people, places, or events are entirely coincidental.

THE WICKED ARE NOT ALLOWED IN THE GARDEN

First edition. December 1, 2024.

Copyright © 2024 Eady H.

ISBN: 979-8230764595

Written by Eady H.

To women everywhere

I stood barefoot on a mirror surrounded by my mother, sisters, and grandmothers, their hands clasped forming a perfect circle. It's the night of my eighteenth birthday and time for my first seed hunt. There's a circular window directly above me and the moon's light shone through bathing my naked body in its glow. Nervous excitement thrummed through me as the women began to hum. The hum turns to a chant, and I take a deep calming breath. This is what I was born to do. Our coven's tradition.

"Hunt the seed. Find the seed," the women chanted as one.

I had waited years to experience this, and I smiled as a purple flame spread around the frame of the mirror. I had watched each of my older sisters go through the ritual of hunting a seed. And they had warned me about the distraction of the first hunt. The feelings and confusion of entering a world that was not mine. Every witch on her eighteenth birthday was sent to earth to lure a male home with her. It's how we furthered our population. And like all the witches before me, it was my turn. A mixture of excited fear churns in my gut.

The chant grew in volume, and I could feel my feet sliding into the mirror as it turned liquid. It's cool as it swallowed my legs and then my waist. Up over my shoulders and still I sink into it. Sliding through it I dropped onto a hard floor landing on my feet with a thud. My sisters had described forests that they had entered through their seed portals, but this place looked sterile.

An alarm started above my head, and I slapped my hands over my ears as I looked around. There's a bed in front of me and a man jumping from it. He slammed into me, and I fell back into a wall. He reached his hand out to steady me and I latched onto him. My first seed. I whipped my head around looking for the portal I came out of and found it above me next to a flashing light. I muttered under my breath, and I rose toward the portal dragging the seed behind me. Just before I entered the portal, I noticed the mark of the wicked on his arm and I let go of him like he'd burned me. He looked up at me with confusion as he fell toward the floor, and I went through the portal.

The alarm sound stopped, and the chanting died out as the women looked down at me standing on the now solid mirror. I looked up at each of them wishing this night had never come. How could the goddess do this to me?

"Mara where is your seed?" my mother asked.

"He was wicked. And the wicked are not allowed in the garden," I said with no emotion. It's the only rule in our home. One must never become with child from a wicked seed.

"Quickly get her into the bath," my mother said to the other women.

My matriarch ushered me into the tub that they fill with herbs for protection and cleansing. I lay there quietly while they lit candles around the basin. Every so often the divine Mother led one of our coven to a wicked seed. All but one of our sisters had been smart enough to not bring her seed back with her. The one who hadn't had been severely punished when the high priestess had found out what she did.

I was in shock over the seed hunt. I was now going to be a maiden forever. Never to take the next step in evolution and become a mother but go straight to crone. Why would the divine have done this to me? Why?

"Come Mara," my mother said with a clap of her hands. "Time to tell the high priestess."

I stepped out of the bath without comment and slipped on one of the thin see-through robes we all wear. What was there to even say? I knew what was next. I would forever be a sister. The only good that could come of that was I had a shot of becoming next high priestess.

Mother led me to the temple which sat on the hill the first coven had arrived on when they had escaped the witch hunts of earth. Led by Mary Elizabeth who had opened a portal to a new world to save her coven from her very own husband. A circle of stone benches surrounded the altar which held a jar of dirt from earth. It sat next to a small statuette of the all Mother. My own mother left me at the edge of the temple and returned home to our waiting family. The next part was all up to me.

The high priestess Estelle sat before the altar, her long brown hair blowing around her in the breeze. The moon glinted off a goblet in her hand as she raised it and poured moon water over her head.

I waited until she lowered the goblet to speak. "Mistress."

Estelle turned to face me with a smile. "Done with your seed already?"

"He's a wick," I said. The words choked me to say as the reality sunk in again. I would never have children.

"Oh honey," Estelle said with a sad smile. "I'm sorry. I know the feeling."

Estelle moved to a stone bench and beckoned me to join her. She took my hand, and we sat silently for a moment. "You're the pride of Mary Elizabeth," Estelle said. "Only those with her strength are tested by the goddess in this way."

I didn't respond as I thought back on the story of Mary Elizabeth, savior of witches. How she hid her coven from her very own husband and left behind her son, afraid he would end up like his father. Men wanted control of women. Wanted them to be docile and meek. They used the sign of the cross to control us. The coven posed a threat to their control, so they started executing women by burning or drowning. Mary Elizabeth opened a portal to the garden so the coven could escape. She was the first high priestess four hundred years ago.

"What do I do now?" I asked. I desperately needed guidance. All I had thought of for years was my seed hunt. Now I would never be a mother. Those things were highly stressed in our world.

Estelle smiled brightly. "I have a job for you."

Dejected, I couldn't think of a job someone like me could do. She tugged me to my feet, and we left the temple and went into the woods. The moon lit our path until the trees got too thick and then Estelle formed a bright ball of energy in her hand. Its light illuminated a path through the dense trees and the path led us to a cabin that was a part of the landscape. The house itself put off strong magic and I could feel it tingling against my skin. Estelle led me inside without knocking. The door opened into a room with a large table overflowing with manuscripts. A middle-aged woman sat at the table diligently writing in one.

"Calysto, I'd like you to meet Mara," Estelle said

"It's been a while since you brought us a new one," Calysto said without looking up.

"I know. Kinda makes you think something is coming doesn't it."

Calysto put down her manuscript and looked up. "No."

Estelle turned to me. "Please tell her what you saw on your seed hunt."

"Uh . . . a room. It was sterile. There was an alarm going off."

"An alarm?" Calysto placed her ink covered fingers on her chin. "Maybe you're right Estelle."

"I'm sorry what's going on? And what does it have to do with my fucked-up seed hunt?"

"It is my belief as it has been my predecessor's belief that the mother chooses some of us to encounter wicks because she wants us to learn from them. Mary Elizabeth always feared they would find a way to the garden."

"How, they can't use magic."

"Yes, but they have something called technology. And it works like magic sometimes," Estelle said.

My head spun. I didn't understand the word technology. How could it be like magic? And why would the wicked use it when they hated us for magic.

"Where do you think all of the eternal sisters go?" Estelle asked.

The eternal sisters were the title women like me bore. Women who would never become mothers because our seeds had been wicked. I had no idea where the eternal sisters went. They just weren't around anymore. A part of me thought maybe when someone stopped coming around that they had moved to a new coven. Or maybe been exiled because of their wicked seed. It's why the term eternal sister held such a terrifying undercurrent. No one knew what happened to them.

"They come here, Mara. They help me study and watch the wicks. I want you to join us. You're the first eternal sister in years. I think the goddess is trying to warn us about something."

"What do I do?"

"In time, I want you to visit your wicked seed so I can find him in my scrying ball and learn his location. But for now, it's been a long night, and I will show you to a room."

Estelle showed me to a room which I guess was my new home. It's so different than what I'm used to, but at least these women understand what it's like to have a wicked seed. A trapped feeling comes over me as I sit on one of many beds in the room. A reminder I'll never be a mother. I've never thought about this reality before. I've always been so caught up in what everyone did, I never stopped to think if that was even what I wanted.

As these thoughts swirl around my head, I stand and stare out the window into the dark. Movement catches my eye outside, and I see a woman exit a portal. It closes behind her and she disappeared into the trees. Curiosity pulled me outside and I attempted to follow her. The full moon's light was choked out by thick trees and there was no light to lead me. The woman's steps were silent as well. I thought about making an orb of light in my hand, but I didn't want her to know I was following her.

"You know it's rude to follow people."

The voice came from behind me, and I whirled around, my heart crashing in my chest. "Goddess, you scared me," I said holding my hand to my breast. "I'm sorry it's just been a bad night." I was ashamed of being caught following a strange witch through the woods. But something had drawn me out here to find her.

"It's okay. I only opened a portal here because I had a premonition about meeting you."

"Can't imagine anyone wanting to meet me after my failed seed hunt." I knew I should just accept it and move on, but in one moment my whole life had ended. I was adrift and I was unsure of my place in the world now.

"Eh, you're not missing much. The male genitalia ain't pretty. All dangly and wrinkly."

"Oh." I'm jealous, I couldn't help it. "How many seed hunts have you been on?" While the male form was not necessarily pleasing to any of us witches, we needed them to make children.

"None. I wasn't raised with the traditions of the garden."

"You're from Earth?" If I was honest the main focus of my own seed hunt had been to see Earth and now, I felt like I was missing out. "How different is it compared to the garden?" It was something I'd heard about so much that I had been looking forward to seeing it for myself. I had never met a witch that had lived on earth before. I knew they existed because the high priestess main task was to find and save witches who needed the garden and a coven to call their own.

"Wana see it?"

"We can just do that?"

"Why not. It's where I just came from."

A little thrill ran through me. I'd never contemplated going to Earth just for the hell of it. Although I knew the high priestess went to save witches still. It was the legacy the first high priestess had handed down. I just kind of assumed Earth was only a place to go if you were finding a seed or a witch in trouble. It had never crossed my mind that Earth was somewhere to go just to have something to do.

Without a comment from me she spread her arms wide, and a portal opened in the air, and I stared in awe. A portal to Earth, with no expectations. I could explore without the task of finding a seed, because I would never again go in search of one of those. She held her hand out to me, and I took it without hesitation. Here this stranger was offering me my dream. She pulled me into the portal and the garden disappeared behind us.

Michael pulled himself from the hard floor and looked up at the corner of his room where he was sure a mostly naked woman had just disappeared. He grabbed his head and shook it; afraid he had cabin fever. He couldn't get her face out of his mind. He held his left arm in his hand and stared at the cross tattoo he had on his forearm. Just before she'd let go, he'd seen a flash of fear in her eyes as she noticed his tattoo. He ran his fingers across his skin before realizing the alarm was blaring in his room. He jumped to his feet and ran to his emergency post.

Exiting his room, he slammed into another body, but the two of them kept going in opposite directions, no time to feel pain. The whole ship was a flurry of activity, people running everywhere. Michael skidded into the security room and saw the captain was already there, shutting off the alarm.

"What gives?" he asked.

She turned and looked at him. "Hull breach."

"Where?" he asked, dropping into his seat and running over the alarm data on one of his screens.

"Not sure, but it was magic. I'm sure of it."

Michael looked around.

"Don't worry Michael. I'm keeping this between the children. If anyone asks it was just a glitch in the system."

"Yes, Aunt Kae. But I agree with you. Magic was in use." Unlike his aunt he had never felt magic, but there was no better reasoning for what had happened in his room. "A . . . a girl came into my room."

"I don't care to hear about this Michael. Your private life is yours," she said turning to leave the room.

"Not like that. Okay maybe like that because she was naked, but she tried to pull me through a hole in my ceiling."

The captain smiled. "Did she now. Did she take you back and get pregnant with your child?"

"No, she freaked out when she saw my tattoo," Michael said holding it up.

A sad smile overtook the captain's face.

"What? What's wrong?"

"Nothing. If you happen to see that girl again, please let me know," Kae said before leaving the security room.

Michael watched her go, unsure what he was missing. Surely his experience was nothing more than space sickness. A hallucination? Whatever it was he couldn't shake the experience from his head. He felt changed somehow. And he really hoped he saw that girl again.

We stepped out onto something solid. A rotting smell swirled around us, and I pinched my nose. "What is that smell?" I asked.

She laughed. "Garbage," she said pointing at containers up against buildings.

For the smell alone I was not impressed with Earth. The sun shone high above us and reflected off of things moving fast at the end of the alley we stood in.

"I'm Surren by the way," she said.

I finally focused on her, and she stole my breath. Her skin was two different colors. Some patches were light, and some were dark. She was also wearing more clothes than I had ever seen another witch wear. She looked more like the seeds I'd seen my sisters bring home. "You're beautiful," I said. "Your skin is so unique."

For the first time since I met her, she seemed slightly embarrassed and rubbed her arms. "It's called Vitiligo."

I smiled at her. "I like it. My names Mara."

She smiled back. "Let me show you my world Mara."

Surren took my hand and led me toward the moving things that reflected the sun. Two impossibly tall buildings rose above us on both sides and I stared up in awe as she led me, my bare feet splashing in stinky puddles.

We stepped from between the buildings and were surrounded by people. More buildings soared above us and there was so much noise I dropped her hand and clamped my hands over my ears. She put her hand on my back and guided me past the fast-moving things and into a building. It was much quieter here and I lowered my hands.

"What were those things? I asked.

"Cars. It's how people get around."

"Can we try one?" As much as I was overstimulated, I was amazed at the things I was seeing. There was nothing like it in the garden.

Surren smiled. "Maybe but first, you need some clothes."

I looked down at myself in the see through robe witches wear then I looked around at the other people who were dressed like her. The clothing was odd because a witch was never clothed. It struck me that these people were hiding in their clothing. Ashamed of bodies the goddess gave them. In the garden no one is self-conscious about their bodies. They are appreciated because they are our houses, a vessel to hold all that we are and will become.

"Pick some clothes," Surren said.

I looked at the shelves unsure where to start. None of it looked comfortable. There were so many colors and patterns and fabrics, I couldn't make sense of the store. "You pick for me." I had no experience at this sort of thing, but part of me also wanted to see what she would choose to cloth my vessel in.

"I was hoping you'd say that," she said with a smile. "You know humans of Earth love style. Everyone has one. Clothes should make a statement."

Surren pulled clothing from racks and ushered me into a little room. I removed my robe and pulled on thigh high stockings, a tiny black skirt and a midriff top. Once I'm dressed, I step out. I'm unsure of myself in this many articles of clothing, but the smile on her face is contagious. Grabbing my shoulders, she turned me so I could see myself in a full-length mirror. Her chin rested on my shoulder smiling at our reflections. I thought I looked unrecognizable, but in a good way.

"You look hot," Surren said.

Little butterflies flit through my stomach at her words. I've crushed on other witches before, but this feels different, more grown up. Perhaps because she's so different. I'd never encountered a witch born on Earth before. We stand like that for a minute, her arms around me and her chin on my shoulder, both of us smiling deliriously at our reflection. And my frustration over my seed hunt no longer seemed to matter. I was just a girl crushing on another girl.

Surren paid for the clothing then took my hand and pulled me from the store. The sounds outside crashed in my ears, and I was instantly overwhelmed again. Surren pulled me to the street and lifted her other hand. A bright yellow car pulled over and she tugged me into the back.

"Luna Park, please," Surren said to the man up front.

I plastered my face to the window of the car and stared out as we drove through town. The buildings rose into the sky, and I found myself mystified by this. Like maybe they were trying to reach their god by building so high. As we pulled up to Luna Park, I'm wowed all over again. Different structures twisted through the air and rose to great heights. Surren pulled me out of the now stopped car, and we looked at the park together.

She led me from ride to ride and stuffed me full of food that tasted amazing. And when the Rainbow wheel stopped at the top, we kissed. It was a perfect day. The lights in the park dazzled me as day turned to night. When the park closed, Surren opened a portal and took us back to the Garden. She kissed me once more outside the cottage then turned and disappeared back into the woods. I smiled as she left, feeling lighter about my situation. I carefully removed the clothing she bought me and placed it under my bed before I lay down.

The next morning when I woke up and went downstairs, Estelle and Calysto were waiting for me.

"Calysto is going to teach you how to astral project. Once you get a handle on it, then I want you to visit the seed in your astral form so I can try and find him in my scrying ball," Estelle said.

I'd almost forgotten about my wicked seed. Surren had succeeded in wiping my failed birthday from my mind and I wished I could go back to last night. With a dejected sigh I followed Calysto back upstairs. I didn't want to astral project back to my failure, I wanted to spend my time with Surren. But I knew the coven's safety came first. That was bred into us since birth. It was why you were never allowed to bring a wicked seed home.

Calysto had me lay down on my bed and close my eyes. "Visualize your body," Calysto said. "Next see yourself stepping outside of it. In front of you is a door. Behind the door is your seed. See it, believe it."

I tried; I really did. But I could hardly get out of my body. Eventually Calysto got frustrated and left the room. I laid there after she left staring at the ceiling feeling like a failure once again. Why couldn't I do this? Frustrated with myself I went outside and sat next to the cottage staring into the woods. Surren emerged and sat next to me.

"Why the long face?" she asked.

"Can't astral project. Calysto isn't happy with me."

"Maybe she's just a bad teacher."

I smiled. "Maybe that's it." She didn't seem like she wanted to be teaching me. She seemed bothered Estelle had asked her to help me.

Surren moved to the ground and patted next to her. "Come on, I'll help."

I lowered myself to the ground and lay down next to her. Surren laid her hand on my forehead and smoothed my hair away. I didn't want to astral project. With her lying next to me stroking my hair my mind went in another direction.

"I know you don't want to see him. But the coven needs to know where he is," Surren said.

I stared up at her as she continued to smooth my hair. I could stay like this all day, but I slid my eyes closed ready to try to astral project. I focused on the feel of her fingers in my hair and let my body relax. She set a hand on my chest and my stomach tingled.

"Let your spirit follow my hand," she said softly.

Little butterflies flittered in my belly then moved lower and I didn't want her hand to leave my chest unless it was sliding lower. Surren's hand slowly lifted from my chest, her fingers felt like they were pulling me up and my spirit drew up and I looked down at our bodies on the ground. Her voice came as if through water and was muffled. Behind her was a door and I knew if I opened it, I would see my wicked seed. I also knew if I'm to open it, then Estelle needed to be here with her scrying ball. I stepped back into my body and as I laid down to rejoin it, I watched the door.

I sat up in my body and smiled at Surren. "I did it. We have to get Estelle."

She sat staring into my eyes with a smile, her hand back in my hair and I leaned forward to kiss her. Her hand tightened in my hair as she kissed me back. The world spun around me until she pulled back.

"We need to tell Estelle," Surren said resting her forehead against mine.

With a deep sigh, I pulled Surren with me as I stood and led her back into the cottage. Estelle was sitting at the table with Calysto who looked annoyed when she saw me. "I did it," I declared looking away from Calysto. "With some help from Surren. Estelle are you ready for me to find the seed?"

Estelle smiled. "Of course."

The group of us went back to my room and I laid down. Like before, Surren sat next to me and stroked my forehead as I closed my eyes. Estelle sat on my other side with a black crystal ball and Calysto stood at the foot of the bed. Surren placed her hand on my chest, and I felt her pull on my astral self and I followed her hand sitting up in my body. I could see myself and the door to the seed in the crystal ball. The door stood at the end of the room.

Slowly I walked toward the door. As my hand wrapped around the handle, I looked back at the others, my body, and the crystal ball. I didn't want to walk through that door. I wanted to put this unfortunate situation behind me and move on with my life. But I turned the handle and stepped through.

The room looked like it did the first time. Bare. My seed was laying in his bed, but this time there were no alarms. I approached the bed and studied the seed. He looked harmless enough, but I knew better. I could see the mark on his arm as he slumbered on, unaware I was standing next to him if only in spirit. I then walked to the door of his room and opened it. Looking both ways outside the door I saw a hallway that stretched for what seemed like forever in both directions. Something called me to exit his room and explore the hallway, but it's lined in doors that look identical to his and I was afraid I wouldn't find my way back to his room and the door that led me back to my body. I closed the door and sat on his bed staring at him while he slept. He's a plain man and I got bored quickly, so I returned to my door. I stepped back into the room where my body was. Calysto was no longer there, and Estelle was wrapping up her scrying ball. Surren was watching my still body. And I allowed myself time to watch her. God, she was gorgeous, and I can't seem to grasp why she'd want to be with someone who had a wicked seed. I watched the way she stroked hair off my face, and I slipped back inside my body so I can feel the sensation of her hands on me. I opened my eyes and looked up into hers.

"I was right," Estelle said. "They're on their way here."

"Now what?" I asked looking over at the high priestess.

"Now we summon the others to the sacred place and tell them what's happening," Estelle said. "Get ready," Estelle said then slipped out of the room.

"Are you coming?" I asked Surren. I didn't want to leave her behind. Whatever was between us I wanted to see where it went.

"Do you want me to come?"

"Yes." I didn't even hesitate, though I'd only known her for a day I found her presence comforting. I knew we would become lovers, but I was hoping we would become partners eventually.

She smiled and took my hand. "Then yes."

The two of us joined Estelle downstairs. She was wearing a satchel on her shoulder and led us from the cottage. I had only ever been to the sacred place when there was a death in the coven. Each witch was placed on the stone of the sacred place and her blood drained into the canals on the rock. Her power was then absorbed by the sacred place.

But it was also a place of community. One where the covens met for solstices and priestess appointments. A witch had to be of partnering age and been on her first seed hunt to participate in these parties at the sacred place. Most importantly was the festival of Lupercalia where the witches usually found their partners.

18 years to the day earlier

Kaelyn laid on her back sweat pouring from her as her stomach and back cramped. She screamed through the gag she'd placed in her own mouth to muffle her cries as her hands twisted the bed sheets under her, while her contraction ripped through her body, and she writhed. Goddess help her, because no one else would. She'd broken the only rule of the coven and been impregnated by a wick. Kaelyn prayed the baby was a girl. Then she could tell them and perhaps they'd show her leniency. The goddess smiled on girls after all.

The door swung open and slammed against the wall. Her partner Estelle stood in the doorway, lightning flashing behind her. Kaelyn hadn't even realized it was storming. Estelle rushed to her side, dropped to her knees, and removed the gag in Kaelyn's mouth.

"My love, why didn't you tell me," Estelle said.

Kaelyn had kept her pregnancy from everyone even her own mother. But Estelle had a way of always finding out her secrets.

"I—" she gritted her teeth as another contraction hit her. "I want a baby." Unfortunately, the goddess had chosen a seed that was wicked.

"My first seed hunt is in another month. What are the odds mine will be wicked. We could still have that family."

"You cannot saddle yourself with an eternal sister. I won't let you." I couldn't imagine my sweet Estelle bound to an eternal sister.

"But I love you. Kaelyn, nothing else matters."

"The only thing that matters to me now is this baby." She hated saying that to Estelle, but Kaelyn couldn't allow Estelle to pay for her choices. She had her own seed hunts and everything else ahead of her.

Estelle took a deep breath as she closed her eyes, but she did not respond. She waited a moment then moved to the foot of the bed. She moved Kaelyn's legs up so she could push the baby out.

"I'm glad you're here," Kaelyn said as another contraction ripped through her. Estelle was the place that felt like home. And it had been sheer torture not telling her about what she'd done.

Estelle placed her hands on Kaelyn's thighs but said nothing.

Kaelyn screamed with the next one and started pushing. When the baby finally came out, she was exhausted and dripping with sweat. But she was awake enough to notice Estelle's frown. "What? What is it? Is my baby, okay?" This was the first time the baby felt like hers.

"It's a boy," Estelle said softly.

Kaelyn hung her head as the baby let out its first wail. The curse of the wick had gotten her. When the coven found out she wasn't sure what they would do. The safety of the coven was above all. "Give him to me."

Estelle swaddled the baby and then placed him in Kaelyn's arms. Kaelyn settled the baby's head against her breast, and he latched on.

She stared down into his little face, and something swelled in her chest. Perhaps this was what it meant to love. She knew then she would leave with the baby. Take a portal to earth or another suitable planet and raise this child apart from the coven that had been her everything since birth. As soon as she was strong enough, she'd take him and leave.

Sleepiness overcame her and her eyes slid closed as she listened to the thunder and the suckling of her child. When she woke Estelle was gone and so was her baby. A sinking feeling settled in the pit of her stomach and bile swelled in her throat. Kaelyn moved with a groan and slowly walked to the door of the one room cottage. She opened it hoping to see Estelle, the woman she loved rocking the baby on the porch watching the rain. But they were not there either.

"Estelle!" she screamed.

The only sounds that came back to her were the steady drip of rain falling from leaves and the roof. She hobbled into the foliage yelling for Estelle. Hoping she would turn up with the baby. Kaelyn heard the babe's cry from ahead of her and she pushed her spent body to move faster. Blood slid down her legs and left a trail on the damp ground providing a trail back to her refuge for anyone looking for her.

"Estelle, give me him please," Kaelyn wailed into the forest. Panic rose inside her and she started breathing heavily. It felt like there was a weight on her chest. *Why would Estelle do this? How could she do this to Kaelyn?*

She continued to chase the sound of her baby's cries through the forest until she emerged at the sacred place. Estelle stood on the stone holding Kaelyn's baby in her arms as he screamed, red in the face. Next to her was the high priestess of their coven and the high priestess of the necromancer coven.

"Estelle, what have you done?" Kaelyn said.

Estelle refused to look at her and ignored the hungry cries of Kaelyn's son.

"We're here to discuss what you have done," the high priestess said.

Kaelyn met her gaze defiantly. Pretending Estelle hadn't just fractured a piece of her heart. "And what of it?"

"You know the rules about procreating with a wicked seed, yet you did. You brought a wicked seed into this garden."

"No, that is the one thing I never did. I followed that rule. My child was conceived on Earth."

"The point is you broke the law. The only law we have."

"I'll take my son, and we'll leave the garden. We'll never come back."

"You will be leaving the garden, yes." The high priestess said as two more witches flanked Kaelyn and grabbed ahold of her arms. "But the baby is another matter entirely."

Estelle handed the baby to the Necromancer. Kaelyn struggled to get free. To get to him. The necromancer held their palm to the baby's face then pulled it backward sucking the soul out of the infant that stilled the minute the soul left its body. Estelle took the limp baby back while the necromancer placed the soul inside of a jar and sealed it. She then placed the jar into her robes and left the sacred place. Kaelyn sagged against her captors and lowered to the ground tears streaming down her face.

"All you had to do was let me leave with him," Kaelyn said.

Estelle still refused to speak. She held the now limp infant almost in disgust.

Kaelyn's captors dragged her to a section of the stone, cut her palms and placed them on the symbols. As they held them there, she felt her power leaving her body. They were stripping her of her magic, and she didn't even have the fight to try to get away. Once she was no longer a witch, the high priestess opened a portal.

"Do not think we did this lightly," the high priestess said. "For we all know the struggles of being presented with a wicked seed. May the goddess smile on you in the next life."

"Give me my baby."

Estelle stepped up next to her. "I hope you know how sorry I am about this outcome. But the wicked are not allowed in the garden. Not even their offspring," she said handing the limp baby to Kaelyn.

The two witches holding Kaelyn pushed her into the portal.

THE WICKED ARE NOT ALLOWED IN THE GARDEN

Power electrified my skin as I stepped from the portal with Estelle and Surren into the sacred place. It was charged with the blood of hundreds of witches who came before. Estelle marched to the center of the stone, pricked her finger and dripped her blood into the grooves marked on it. A white bird made of smoke came out of the stone and rose in the air. With a flap of its wings, it headed over the garden to spread Estelle's summons to the other high priestesses.

We didn't have long to wait until portals were opening all around us and the high priestesses from the other covens enter the sacred place. They gathered with Estelle at the center. I'm unsure if I should join them so I hung back with Surren. Every so often the other witches cast glances at me, and it made me uncomfortable. I hadn't chosen a wicked seed. The goddess had done that to me. My body was strung with tension as they continued their talk. Surren took my hand and led me into the forest while the high priestesses discussed the situation facing the whole garden.

"They don't really need us to stay," Surren said.

I wasn't so sure. Why would Estelle have brought me if she didn't still want something from me? Maybe I just wanted to feel needed.

"There's nothing wrong with you, Mara. The goddess chose you for a reason."

I gave Surren a small smile. I knew she meant well. And it was nice to hear, but Surren had not been given a wicked seed. And sure, had I not gotten that seed, then the garden would not have known the wicked were coming for them. I just wished it hadn't been me. Now I needed a new path.

Surren stroked the back of my hand with her thumb and the world narrowed to the two of us. Nothing else mattered but the way she was looking at me. Like she really saw me. Not what I should have been, but what I am.

"You wanna get out of here?" Surren asked.

I wanted to tell her yes. I didn't want to be here anymore, but I felt like I also needed Estelle's blessing to leave since she was my high priestess. Before I could make up my mind or respond, Estelle found us.

"We have decided to monitor the situation, and each coven is going to prepare separately for the impending invasion," Estelle said.

"Um, what's my role?" I asked.

Estelle stared at Surren and I's clasped hands. "You will always have a home with the eternal sisters. But I want you to have the freedom to live the life you choose. Especially before things change."

"Do you really think the wicked will change things?" I asked. I knew they were coming, but they had no magic. How could they possibly hope to conquer us?

"We must never underestimate our enemy. Take what time the goddess gives."

Estelle gave us both a smile then left and a weight I didn't know I was carrying went with her. I was no longer responsible for the wick's actions.

Surren squeezed my hand and pulled me to my feet. "Where to?"

"I don't know." As free as the life of a witch was, I'd never left my own coven. I'd never seen the rest of the garden. But the allure of Earth was pulling on me too. "I've never been anywhere but the coven I was born into." Admitting that to her made me feel a little bit of shame. She seemed so worldly and I'm not. It made me worry I won't be enough for her.

Surren smiled. "The worlds are our oyster."

I'm not sure what an oyster is but I'd follow her wherever she led. It's not the path I had been raised to envision, but in this moment it felt right.

Kaelyn huddled up against a cold building, her dead son in her trembling arms, sounds and smells assaulting her. She shivered as cold rain ran across her skin. For the first time in her life, she knew fear. Earth was dirty and loud and alien. Without her magic she was unprotected in a world that wanted her dead. And without her son, she wasn't even sure she wanted to live.

She'd been raised to trust the goddess. To avoid the wicked. To procreate. And while she had not avoided the wicked, the goddess had sent her there. And she'd hoped to glorify the goddess with her offspring. But now she was ruined. A husk. No child, no magic. And where was the goddess in all of this? Could she not show herself in this moment? Kaelyn needed her.

Emptiness consumed her as she clutched her baby to her chest. She truly had nothing now. And while she could recognize her part in her current situation, she burned with hatred for Estelle. The one person who should have been there for her had turned her in and cost her child his life. Her hatred was the only thing keeping her going because she really wanted to lie down next to her child and die.

Kaelyn spent the night huddled in the corner of an alley. When the sun finally rose, she could hardly move, her muscles were so stiff. Blood from the birth still coated her legs and was still coming out of her. Her naked body was cold, and she could barely keep her eyes open. She forced herself to her feet and shambled forward. She needed to find warmth. She needed to find help. She needed a hug. Tears slipped from her overtired eyes and dripped down her dirty face. She walked until she couldn't anymore, and she collapsed to the ground still clutching her baby's body. Her eyes were heavy, and she tried to keep them open as shapes blurred above her.

Estelle watched Surren and Mara disappear into the forest. Calysto came out of a portal and stepped up next to her.

"You're really letting her leave with Surren?" Calysto asked.

"She's made a choice and I'm going to honor that." She'd learned from past mistakes. Everyone had a choice over their life. They could be more than what their traditions taught.

"But you know who her mother is."

"Who her mother was."

"And still you let Mara leave with her. Why?"

"Calysto have you ever been in love?" Estelle asked.

"Of course not."

Estelle sighed. Most of the witches did not want an eternal sister as a partner. They were seen as less. Something the goddess had turned their back on yet elevated enough they were chosen to be high priestess. It's why Estelle had built the cabin in the woods for others like herself. "Then you won't understand what a person would do for love."

"They just met," Calysto said.

"Time is not a measurement of love. Surren came along when Mara needed someone. Whether that was constructed by Surren remains to be seen. But Mara will have to go on her own discovery of Surren's identity."

"You should have never let Surren enter the garden."

"She was a witch in trouble. It is my duty as a high priestess to save witches. Even those who were in the care of someone who hates us. She's a powerful witch and she has as much cause as us to hate the wicked."

"I don't trust her."

"She has nothing to do with the wicked coming here."

Estelle and Calysto returned to the cabin the eternal sisters lived in. Calysto went back to her manuscripts while Estelle went to her room. She uncovered her scrying ball and once more she looked in it for Kaelyn. Estelle regretted her actions in Kaelyn's exile and the death of her son. She should have never told the high priestess. But like always she couldn't find her. It had taken her months after Kaelyn had been exiled to even try. And then there was just nothing. She truly hoped her beloved was okay.

Surren led me through the garden, her hand wrapped around mine. Almost absentmindedly her thumb stroked my hand. I had no idea where we were going but I didn't care. I was with her. Something about her excited me. We walked hand in hand for hours just talking. She did most of it and I learned about her life on Earth. Her birth mother had been a witch, and she had taught her from a young age how to harness her power, yet what they were was kept secret from her father. Although one day he discovered her mother's secret and killed her. Not long after he had remarried, and her father and stepmother had made her life hell until she had finally been saved. She didn't elaborate on that, but I assumed it was when a high priestess had saved her and brought her to the garden. As the day wound down Surren led me to a small cabin in the forest.

"This is my home," Surren said.

I was amazed, as witches are usually not solitary creatures. "You didn't join a coven?"

"I'm never living under someone else's ideas again. I understand the coven's rules, and I don't begrudge them doing what makes them feel safe. This is what makes me feel safe."

My heart broke for her. She'd only ever had her mother, where the witches here had their entire matriarchal line to help raise them. She experienced what Mary Elizabeth had tried to spare us all from. Hatred. I'd never met my father because once a witch became pregnant the seed was returned to Earth. This was all Surren had left to herself, and she trusted me enough to show it to me.

We spent the evening sitting on the front porch watching the sun go down and then curled up together on her bed where we fell asleep talking. In my dreams I saw the door that led to my wicked seed. There was a strong pull to open the door, and I struggled with the desire to open it. The door beckoned to me like a siren. Answering the call, I opened the door and entered the wick's bedroom.

The bed was empty and the door to his room drew my eye. My focus narrowed on it, and I crossed the space and opened the door. The hallway stretched into the distance to the left and right, but something called me to the right. Almost like a thrumming I could feel inside myself and I followed the urge passing door after door. The hallway curved and as I rounded it, I caught sight of a woman standing at the other end of the hall. She wore the garments of a witch, so out of place on the ship of the wicked.

I hesitated and she smiled at me. She was older, perhaps around the age of my high priestess. The thrumming feeling was coming from her direction, and I noticed she held something in her hands. It was a small cauldron, but I felt the pull of it. It called to my spirit. Before I could move forward anymore, I heard Surren calling my name. I felt my body jerk backward and fly toward the seed's room. Surren's voice pulled me through the doorway and back into her cabin.

I opened my eyes to see Surren leaning over me. Before she masked it, I saw worry in her eyes. "Was I snoring?" I asked.

She smiled. "No. What do you want to do today?"

Kaelyn woke on a cloud, things beeping around her. A horrible sterile smell clogged her nose. When she moved, she felt a sharp pain in her hand, and she looked down to see a tube coming out of the back of her hand. Clear liquid dripped through it into her veins. She realized her son was missing from her arms and she moved her hands over the blanket that covered her hoping to find him. A throat cleared and she stilled before turning her head toward the noise. A man stood there in a blue uniform watching her.

"Where is my baby?" she asked.

"I'm sorry ma'am your baby was deceased when we found you. It's currently in the hospital morgue."

"Hospital?"

"You were very sick when we found you on the street."

Kaelyn started to cry. It didn't matter where she was now. She had nowhere to go in a world that was not hers. She didn't even have her magic to help her. And now her baby was gone completely. "I want him back. I want my baby back."

"I'm sorry ma'am. He's not coming back. The hospital can set you up with a grief counselor. And I know this is going to be painful, but I have to ask. What happened to him?"

He was betrayed. How could a counselor understand the grief of the girl she loved ripping out her heart and murdering her son? "He was stillborn." She knew a man would never understand what had happened to her. She needed to find other witches. She needed a coven.

Before the man could respond, another knocked on the door and stepped inside. This man she recognized. Her wicked seed. Kaelyn clenched her fists.

"It is you," he said.

"Who are you?" the man in uniform asked.

"Uh . . ." he said. "Jeff."

"And who are you to her?"

"The baby's father," Kaelyn said.

"Ah. I'll give you guys some time. I'll be back later to follow up," he said before stepping out of the room.

Jeff closed the door behind him and moved to the chair by the bed. "Is our son . . ."

"Dead?"

Jeff cringed at the word.

"Yes." The goddess had deserted her.

"What happened to him?"

"My coven found out about him." Kaelyn hadn't seen Jeff since she'd confirmed she was pregnant. While seeds were brought back to the garden until they impregnated the witch who had brought them back. She had never brought him into the garden because he was wicked. But she had told him about where she was from. About their rules. About why she needed him. But she'd never told him he was different from the other seeds. "Because he's yours."

"Why would they kill him? What have I done?"

"That," Kaelyn said as she pointed at the tattoo on his forearm.

He looked down. "The cross?"

"Men of the cross hunted down our ancestors and burned them at the stake," she said and laid her head back against the pillow, hot tears on her cheeks.

"I'm not a man of the cross. I was in the military. Everyone has one."

She sniffed. "It doesn't matter. The wicked are not allowed in the garden. Not even their sons. I broke the law. I got him killed when he should have never been conceived."

"Kaelyn, believing in God makes me no more wicked than you being a witch. Our child deserved to live. Now you take me to this garden of yours and I will take vengeance for our son."

"I can't. They took my powers. I'm stuck on Earth." She had no powers, no home, and no child. She was truly alone in the world now.

Surren and I spent the day watching movies in a theatre and making out in the back row. Her mouth tasted like sugar and was just as addicting. She made me giddy, and my toes curl. I no longer had a dark cloud hanging over my head over my failed seed hunt. I was living for every moment with her. But as fantastic as my day was, when I went back to sleep, the seed called to me in my dreams. Like the night previous, the door sat at the end of the bed, and I went through it. Again, his room was empty, and I felt a pull into the hall. I followed the feeling to the end of the hall where the same woman was standing there.

"Who are you?" I asked.

"Someone just like you. Betrayed by the goddess. Given a wicked seed."

My stomach clenched at her words. Even though I had found Surren, and she kept my mind from it, I was still tainted by it. "Why do you bring me here?"

"Because I need your help."

Before I can respond or she can tell me what kind of help, I hear Surren calling to me and I fly backward all the way back to my body and open my eyes to Surren. Her eyes look worried again, like she knew where I'd been.

She wrapped her arms around me and tucked her head into my neck, her breath hot on my skin. "Where do you go when you're sleeping?"

I was quiet for a moment as I thought about her question. I didn't want to lie to her, but I don't like where I've been. "The ship."

"With your seed?"

"Yes, but he's not there when I go. There's this woman. She's holding something that draws me to her. And she's dressed like a witch. She said she needs my help."

"I don't think you should trust her. After all she's with a wick. That can't be good," Surren said as she squeezed me tighter.

"Yeah," I said softly. "She's probably no good."

Surren snuggles deeper into me, and I hold her back. Every time I'm drawn to the ship, she pulled me back and kept me grounded. Soon Surren was snoring in my ear, but I couldn't go back to sleep. Despite the fact that I agreed with her that the woman was no good. A seed had been planted inside of me and I was curious what she wanted. Why she called to me? How she knew about the wicked seeds?

Kaelyn left the hospital with Jeff; her arms empty of their baby. She was hollow inside. Forced to trust and rely on a wick because her own people had deserted her. He took her to his sad little one room apartment. Its location in the middle of the city suffocated her. There was no greenery, no signs of life. Everything a witch needed to thrive. On top of that Jeff bought her clothing that covered her entire body which furthered the suffocating feeling she had.

Jeff seemed to think that she was his now. Proof that he was in fact wicked. He droned on and on about a family. About her place in the home. It served to steel her nerves and helped her decide she was going to find other witches still on Earth.

Kaelyn spent months pretending to be a dutiful wife. A role that was so much different here than it was in the garden. There, wives were partners. They shared the load. Here, the man made something he called money that paid for items and their home while the woman was expected to keep the home. She resented it and him, but she had to pretend so he would fulfill her needs to find sisters and form a new coven. Because she was going back to the garden, and she was going to release her son's soul.

She started small at first. Recruiting children, adopting them from the streets and teaching them about her life in the garden. She made them loyal. She hoped for some witches among them but was disappointed. Once she had a loyal group of children, she started looking for witches who needed saved. She hoped to reach them before the high priestess. Jeff eventually moved them to a large country house where she could raise the children and house the witches. The first witch she recruited she had, use a spell to hide her from the prying eyes of the garden priestesses, and her beloved Estelle. Her now mortal enemy.

When Surren woke up, we decided to stay in the garden as opposed to returning to Earth. We spent part of the morning lounging in bed exploring each other's bodies. As the afternoon light filtered through her windows, we finally climbed from bed.

"I want to show you something," Surren said.

"Okay," I said with a smile. She always had something to show me, and I loved learning from her.

Surren took my hands and closed her eyes. I left mine open and watched as her little cabin disappeared and was replaced with a lake. Wind blew through our hair and water lapped at our ankles. I looked around amazed.

"How did you do that?" I asked.

Surren opened her eyes and smiled. "This is a place I created after my mother passed away. A safe space from my father and his second wife."

Behind Surren sat a cabin which overlooked the lake we stood in. "How did you make all of this?"

"Belief. Belief makes things real. You need to learn that."

The phrasing of Surren's statement gave me pause as she took my face in her hands and looked deep into my eyes. I could feel how serious her request was, but I couldn't explain why. She kissed my forehead then pulled me deeper into the lake.

As we swam, snow drifted out of the sky. The water remained warm even with the cold pricks landing on our skin, the feelings making me delirious. Surren was the most wonderful thing I had ever encountered, let alone got to call mine. Every minute I spent with her was a gift. Perhaps the goddess had set up the wicked seed so I could meet Surren.

We spent the rest of the day in her safe space. I was honored that she would show me something so personal. That night we fell asleep in a hammock on the porch of the cabin and the door was waiting for me once more. I try to ignore it, but the strength of its pull is overwhelming. Through the door, down the hall like every other time. But this time the woman isn't at the end of the hall. The pull leads me through a door at the end of the hall and down a set of stairs to a large, cavernous room. The woman is standing there, a smile on her face.

"Welcome back. We have much to discuss."

"What do you need my help with?"

"Finding my son."

"What are you?" I asked because witches did not have sons.

"A witch who had a child with a wicked seed."

I remembered hearing about a witch who got pregnant with the child of a wicked seed, growing up. Everyone had heard the tale. Mothers used it to reinforce to their daughters that they did not bring a wicked seed home. But wicked seeds were rare.

"You broke the rules," I said.

"What would you do for a child? The one thing that is drilled into a young witch's head. Become a mother."

While this woman believed that was the only function of a witch, she was also missing the rest of our way of life. It was community, harmony, natural. True, she had also felt the pressure of the seed hunt to procreate. The burn of that was what had hurt about being given a wicked seed. The fact that she would never be a mother. But she'd found someone who wanted her anyway. That thought kept her from buying in to the woman before her.

"The garden comes first. And the wicked are not allowed in the garden. Not even their offspring," I said.

The woman scoffed. "That rule cost me my son."

"You cost you your son. He should never have been created. And while I can't fault you for craving a child since it is what we're taught, I can fault you for being dumb about it. When you got pregnant you should have left. So, you cost you your son."

The woman's face contorted in anger, but I felt no fear because I heard Surren calling me. And I thought I would soon be out of there, but my body didn't move. The woman cackled.

"She can't reach you anymore," the woman said.

Suddenly I was worried. I was in my astral form, I couldn't use magic, and she must truly be powerful to trap an astral body, something intangible.

Surren shook Mara's body and begged her to wake up. Every time before calling her name had worked, but this day she couldn't get her to rouse.

Surren took Mara in her arms and opened a portal which she carried her through. Surren stepped into the house of eternal sisters and found Estelle and Calysto sitting at the table covered in manuscripts.

"Help her," Surren said.

"What did you do to her?" Calysto asked.

Surren ignored her and looked at Estelle. "She's been drawn to the ship every night. Usually when I call her it pulls her back. But last time she said she met with a woman. A witch. And we both know who is captain of that ship."

"Lay her down," Estelle said gesturing at the table.

Calysto sighed loudly as Mara was laid on top of the manuscripts. Estelle moved to stand at her head and moved her hands around Mara's skull with her eyes closed.

"I can't feel her in there," Estelle said opening her eyes. "Calysto, I need you to astral project and find her. Figure out how to get her back in her body."

"I told you not let Mara leave with her," Calysto said. "You think she didn't have something to do with this."

"I would never do anything to hurt Mara. Most especially to help that woman."

"Calysto please. We cannot leave a fellow witch behind."

Calysto grudgingly tipped her head back and closed her eyes. Estelle and Surren stood watching both of them tensely. Time ticked on and neither of them opened their eyes. Estelle began to pace.

"Get your scrying ball," Surren said.

"She's blocked my view of her. If they are indeed with her, then I won't be able to see them."

"Fuck," Surren said then opened a portal. To save Mara, she was going to jeopardize their relationship. She stepped onto the ship and strode to the hold. There she found Mother Kae, Surren, Calysto.

"Darling, fancy meeting you in a place like this," Kae said.

Mara's head whipped toward Surren as Calysto said, told ya so.

Surren kept her eyes from Mara. "I'm going to need my girlfriend back. And that other bitch."

"Girlfriend? You left me for the Garden?"

Surren had been saved when she was younger, but not by the high priestess. Instead Kae had been the one to save her. She brought her to her compound, where the boys called her Aunt Kae, and the girls called her mother. Surren hadn't been looking for another mother, but she had been grateful to have been saved from her stepmother.

Kae had always told them stories of the garden. Stories of her own rejection and dismissal from it for having the child of a wicked seed. As Surren had aged and seen more of Kae's plans, she realized had Kae not taken her, the high priestess would have eventually saved her and taken her to the garden. After she realized that she'd grown to hate Kae for taking away her chance of being there. Of being safe. Kae had broken a very simple rule and been cast out. Surren had left and entered the garden on her own. Hoping to never have to return to the safe place she'd created. A place she had still visited while being raised by Kae.

"Wasn't a hard choice. The garden has expected nothing of me." Kae had always expected the witches in her care to share their power with her.

"Not even a child? I know how much you've wanted to be an eternal sister."

"I make my own rules, Kae. And I follow the simple one you couldn't."

"Do you think that gives them the right to do what they did to me?"

"No, but that's between you and Estelle. Now give me my girlfriend." Surren had tried to urge Kae over the years to have it out with Estelle. She'd even offered to open a portal for her. But the woman refused. She wanted to see the whole garden suffer.

"Tell you what," Kae said. "You bring me the soul of my son and I'll give you both of them."

"You swear?"

"On my son."

Not sure she believed that, Surren cut her hand and held it out to Kae. "On your blood."

Kae cut her hand and shook Surren's. Blood was binding so Kae couldn't go back on her word. Surren chanced a glance at Mara who wouldn't meet her eyes. Calysto glared at her, but before she could object to Surren retrieving the soul of the child Surren walked through a portal. She came out in the village of the necromancers. She'd briefly toured it upon her entry to the garden because she had been curious about Kae's baby's soul. She'd noticed it and several others in the temple of the necromancers. All of them were labeled. None of the necromancers paid Surren any mind as she walked into their temple now and picked up the jar that contained Kae's son's soul. With a flick of her hand another portal opened, and she walked into it carrying the jar.

Kae, Mara, and Calysto were where she had left them, and she handed it to Kae hesitantly.

"My, my, that was fast. Almost like you knew where it was."

"I've known where it's been for years. Now honor our deal."

Kae waved her hand as she looked longingly at the soul in the jar. "They're free to go."

"Stay away from the garden," Surren said as she tried to take Mara's hand.

Mara yanked her hand back and walked back to her body. Calysto followed her silently. For the first time in a long time, Surren felt hurt. It was her own fault she knew, but still, Mara's rejection stung.

"She'll never love you now," Kae said. "Might as well come back to me and your siblings."

"You people are not my family," Surren said as she opened a portal. Once it was all she'd wanted to be part of Kae's family. At first it had looked like a great safe place to be. But she'd eventually seen through the façade.

Surren hid in the special place she had made for herself. Her dad was drunk again, and his wife had smacked her in the face for telling her she wasn't her mom. Surren had been young when her mother died, but she remembered her. How she taught her to weave spells and commune with nature. Her mother had helped her to create the safe space Surren now used as a refuge.

She liked to imagine her mother was in the cabin making dinner while Surren splashed in a lake that was always a comfortable temperature. They'd both come there when her dad was drunk and angry. Although the last time, her mother had not gotten to the safe space in time. Surren had buried her under the tree to the left of the house.

When she had returned to her father's house, Kae was sitting in her room. "Hello Surren. I've a proposition for you."

"How did you get in my room?" Surren asked. She always locked her door so her stepmother and drunken father couldn't sneak up on her in her sleep.

Kae smiled. "Magic."

"There's no such thing," Surren said. Her mother had taught her to deny it because most people either didn't believe or would harass you if they did.

"You don't need to hide your gifts from me," Kae said. "I'm a witch like you and I have a safe space for others like us. No more hiding from people who don't get you. Would you like to come live with me?"

Surren didn't want to let herself hope that there was a place where someone like her could be free. But anywhere had to be better than here. "I'll try it."

Kae smiled. "That's all I ask. If you'll pack, we can go."

Surren threw her clothes in a bag. There was nothing else from this house she wanted. There weren't even any pictures of her mother in it.

Kae took Surren's hand, and they left the room. Surren looked around for her father and stepmother but didn't see either of them as they went through the house and out the door. Kae led her to a car. Behind the wheel was a man Kae introduced as Jeff. In the backseat was a girl, Kae called Leti who she would later find out was a witch like her.

They took Surren to a property in the middle of nowhere that had several buildings. One looked like a regular two-story farmhouse, the other two were long buildings. Kae explained the boys lived in one and the girls lived in the other. The girls and boys were not to interact, which was fine with Surren, because she didn't like boys in any capacity. She'd find out later that Kae no longer had her powers and why.

Surren went into training with the other girls to use their magic offensively. Kae wanted to take over the garden. To upset the society the high priestesses had built. For years she had trained and studied and believed in the mission, but one day, she'd seen the mark of the wicked on one of the boys. Surren had told the boy, the wicked are not allowed in the garden, but the boy didn't seem to understand what she was saying.

It was then Surren realized the boys and girls were taught different things. She didn't bother to talk to Kae about it, she'd just packed her bag and disappeared. Not long after Estelle had found her and brought her to the garden where she had lived alone until she'd had a premonition about Mara.

I sat up on the table in the eternal sister's home as Calysto lifted her head. Estelle looked relieved as Surren walked out of a portal.

"You bitch," Calysto said.

"Mara, I—"

"I'm going home Estelle. I need to see my family," I said hopping off the table. I needed time to think. I walked past Surren without looking at her and she didn't try to follow me. I went back to the house I had been raised in by my mother and her partner. Where I had watched numerous sisters go on their first seed hunt. Where they had met their partners and started their own matriarchs. Where I had dreamed my life would be the same. Where those very hopes had been dashed.

When I walked through the door it was as if no time had passed in my absence. My mothers were cooking and laughing in the kitchen while my youngest sister practiced spells. When my natural mother noticed me, she looked at me with a sad hesitant smile and I walked into her embrace. I'd missed her. Missed the simpleness of girlhood. Tears smarted my eyes and fell onto her shoulders and into her hair.

She rubbed my back. "We've missed you."

I sniffed. "I missed you guys too."

We hugged a moment longer before she ushered me into a seat and my other mother set a cup of tea in front of me before moving to my natural mother's side and looked expectantly at me. So, I told them what had happened since the night of my seed hunt that felt like a lifetime ago. About the witch who was coming here because she had been exiled. About Surren and how she had made me feel, and how much it had hurt when I found out what she had been keeping from me.

After my tale, we had dinner, then I went to bed in my old room. And for the first time in a while I went nowhere in my dreams. I slept peacefully and when I woke in my bed alone the next morning sadness engulfed me. Despite my hurt, I still wanted to wake up next to Surren.

I was still lying in bed dejected when I heard an odd noise outside. I got up and looked out my window. Large spheres blasted through the sky and slammed into the ground. Shock waves of dirt collapsed houses. And rocked mine rattling the windows. I ran downstairs screaming for my mothers'. Their panicked faces greeted me when I stepped off the stairs. The three of us left our home and went toward the houses that had collapsed. More and more witches filled the streets of our village and used our power to lift pieces of houses and aid those who had been injured and removed those who had been killed.

Sometime during the situation Estelle had emerged from the forest to help, and she gathered us up when the work was done. "Ladies, we are under attack by the wicked, led by our very own outcast Kaelyn. I think it wise we retreat to the sacred place, where we are more powerful."

We followed the high priestess carrying our dead to the sacred place. The walk was slow as we mourned those we'd lost in the first wave of the attack. We would normally use a portal, but the dead deserved the long slow walk of mourning. The stillness of the garden was punctuated by more objects punching through our atmosphere and screaming toward the ground. By the time we reached the sacred place other covens had come with their own dead to place upon the stone.

The patterned stone was almost completely covered as we all sat around it and joined hands. Power thrummed through us as we hummed awakening the stone. It drank greedily from our dead and grew in power, the feel of it like a weight on our skin. Before we could remove their now empty bodies and cast them out into the universe through a portal, Kaelyn herself strode into the sacred place. On her chest was the glass jar holding her son's soul. Black tendrils wrapped around her coming from the jar.

Her 'family' of witches strode from the trees to surround us as she moved among our now empty dead. "Estelle, come out, come out wherever you are."

Estelle stood from left her place along the stone and walked toward Kaelyn. "Here, I am love. Now leave our sisters be."

"My sisters," Kaelyn scoffed. "The same women who stood by while you and the high priestess took my son's soul and cast me out?"

"I'm sorry, for what I did to our . . . your son. I deserve everything you've thought of and more for what I put you through."

"You're damn right, Estelle. Your betrayal will be punished. But you are not the only one who wronged me."

"I'm the only one left alive to punish," Estelle said.

Kaelyn laughed. "The rest are right under our feet." She bent and caressed the stone, her magic returning to her as she rubbed her fingers over the carvings. She inhaled it into herself and the dead around her stood to their feet.

Estelle shook her head. "Don't do this."

"Witches, you are to leave this space. It is no longer yours. And before you think you are going to use magic against me, the sisters I brought with me are just as powerful as you, but quicker to use their power to murder. Good luck in the forest where the wick's will be making their own town to live in your garden."

There was murmuring among the covens as the dead started forcing us out of the sacred space. I felt a set of arms go around me and then I had the sensation of falling and the sacred place was replaced by the necromancer's village. I turned and saw Surren behind me.

"We have to go back," I said.

"She's too powerful right now. She's siphoning power from the soul of her son. His magic is fresh, untapped potential because he's never used any of it. We need more power. And where else can we get some, but here."

Surren led me inside the necromancer's temple where there were souls in jars.

"Why would they do this to people?" I asked.

"Not every witch believes in harmony. There are those who desired to return to Earth and attack the wicked for their ancestor's role in driving us from the Earth," the high priestess of the Necromancers said joining us.

"So now what?" I asked.

"Now you have to agree with this. Because it's going to be painful, and it may not be reversable."

"I can't do it, or I would," Surren said. "I'm not of the garden so I cannot join with one of these souls."

I wasn't really sure what I was agreeing to and didn't feel like I had time to ask. "Will this help stop her?"

"Oh yeah."

"Do it."

The high priestess selected a jar from the wall and carried it to the front of the temple. "Stand here," she said pointing at the center of a circle on the floor.

I did as she asked, and she handed me the jar and exited the circle. Her and Surren stood around the edges of the circle and five more witches joined them.

"Open the jar," the high priestess said.

They held hands, tipped their heads back and started mumbling words I couldn't quite hear. I opened the lid and the soul inside slowly rose out of the jar. It drifted around my body as the witches chanted. It slid around my body and hovered against my lips. I sucked in and the smoky substance slid down my throat. I could feel it threading through my nerves and power I didn't recognize pulsed through me. My veins screamed and my skin split, fire spilling out of me and coating my body. I dropped to my knees in pain as this soul fused with mine, a voice screaming in my mind. The chanting stopped as I collapsed to the ground, exhausted as two became one. I laid there for a moment catching my breath before climbing to my feet. I could feel the other soul in the back of my mind, but I ignored it because we both had one goal. To kill what didn't belong in the garden. I stepped out of the circle and Surren reopened the portal for me.

On the other side Kaelyn still stood on the stone of the sacred place. Estelle was on her knees before her with her hands tied. The dead witches' empty bodies stood keeping the covens away while Kaelyn's witches chanted. Beside Estelle two forms were growing out of the stone. One was Mary Elizabeth, and one was the High priestess before Estelle. Fire flashed down my arms and I rushed at Kaelyn. She turned and caught my first fist, but my other one slammed into the jar where her son's soul was housed and cracks webbed outward. A dark blast from her chest knocked me backward and I met it with more flames. While the two forces pushed against each other, Surren stepped from a portal and threw a lasso of power over Kaelyn's head and drew it tight choking her. Kaelyn's hands went up to grab the rope, and my fire no longer held off slammed into her and melted the jar into her skin. Her shrill screams made hoarse by the noose of power Surren wielded.

The soul in the jar exploded from her chest and the blast knocked all three of us off our feet rolling me across the stone of the sacred place. I felt something in my throat and wretched up the soul I'd swallowed. It dissolved into the stone, and I struggled to my feet as my skin bled from where the flames had split me open. Kaelyn was on her knees, her chest and face charred, skin hanging off in seared bits.

"I just wanted my son," Kaelyn shrieked as her witches chanting faltered.

Estelle struggled to her feet and approached Kaelyn. She crouched next to her and rested her head against hers. "I am sorry my love."

Kaelyn's blood dripped down into the stone, and she fell sideways. Estelle laid down next to her and pulled her dead mutilated body to her chest and wept. Surren approached me, my own blood dripping from where the fire had ripped out of me.

"I'm sorry for not telling you everything about my past," Surren said. "I should have said something about her. And I know it looks like I used you to get to her son, but I didn't know about your seed hunt when I had the premonition about meeting you. And then I didn't want to tell you because I didn't want you to think my interest insincere."

I looked at her, the girl who had stolen my days, and loved me through my disappointing seed hunt. The girl who had shown me the Earth I had romanticized. The girl who made my insides squishy, and I pulled her into my arms and kissed her.

No matter what happened now that life in the garden had been wrent in half. I had her. And somewhere out there in the garden was my wicked seed. But the wicked were not allowed in the garden, so something told me for a while at least, the meaning of seed hunt was going to be entirely different than what I had grown up knowing it to be.

Michael had watched the invasion from the ground. Kae had insisted he be with her when she portaled to the garden. Their ship was above the planet launching projectiles toward the surface, aimed near the villages. Kae took most of the witches with her. She was sure the residents of the garden would retreat to a place of power to protect themselves. While the garden was distracted by her, Michael was supposed to invade the village Kae had grown up in. A few witches were on the ship opening portals for the men to come onto the planet.

Once they were all on the ground, the witches took control and led the men to the village Kae had indicated. The witches made sure the town was empty before the men came in. This was the promised land Kae had told them about.

They were busy assigning homes when the witches called for them to gather outside. Michael noticed the witches that were with Kae portaling into the town. They looked scared.

Michael edged closer and heard them saying Kae was dead. They all seemed shocked, like she was infallible to them. But Michael knew what it meant. They were no longer protected by the threat of Kae. The residents of this planet would be coming for them. And while the rest were not self-aware enough to vacate, he was. This village would have a giant target on its back. And they were all sitting ducks.

Michael slipped away unseen into the surrounding forest. He'd been on his own once, he could do it again. For two days he foraged and tried to think of a way to convince the women of this planet not to kill him. He was still trying to figure that out when he stumbled upon a cabin all by itself in the forest. Since everyone else on this planet seemed to be all about community, he hoped this cabin was empty. He cautiously approached but stopped short when the girl from his room walked out of the cabin holding hands with Surren. Both of them stopped short when they saw him.

"What are you doing here, Michael?" Surren asked.

"How do you know my wicked seed?" Mara asked.

"Because we were raised by the same woman," Surren said. "You need to leave Michael."

"And go where? The ship won't work without the witches, and even if it did, I can't get to it." He couldn't believe the girl from his room had ended up with Surren.

"I'll send you back to it," Surren said.

Michael sighed. He knew he shouldn't expect a warm welcome. Afterall, she had told him so very long ago that the wicked are not allowed in the garden.

"We just wanted a place to call our own," he said.

"You can't do that by taking something that's not yours," Surren said.

"Send me back to Earth."

With a wave of her hand, Surren opened a portal. "Be free of Kae."

I watched my wicked seed enter the portal to Earth and disappear and I hoped the rest of the covens had as easy of a time with any wicked they encountered. But there was something he had said that stuck in my mind.

"Can we go see the ship?" I asked.

Surren shrugged. "Why not."

Surren opened a portal, and we entered it hand in hand. Physically I had only been here once, but my astral and dream form had visited the ship several times. This time was different. There was a heaviness in the air that made it feel cold and dead. I finally understood the word technology. It was magic that was empty and unfeeling unlike ours which was natural and in communion with the world around us.

Surren and I wandered through the empty space, and I pitied the people who had journeyed in such a vessel. The walls began to shrink in on me and I asked Surren to return us to our home. The little cabin we would grow old in together, surrounded by nature.

Estelle sat on our porch waiting for us as we stepped from the portal. She met us halfway to the house. "The wicked have scattered throughout the garden, while Kaelyn's coven have disappeared. Tonight we hunt the wicked."

Mother Fuckin women
cursed
by the gift of a rib
blessed
by a bite of the fruit
the man is in us
the man thinks he owns us
believed to be soft
accused of more
blood of the virgin
blood of the whore
defy all patriarchies
kiss those serpents
Luci fee
Luci fi
we are temptress
we are creators
we are goddesses
we're an ecosystem
we are
Mother fuckin women

The Earth Swallows

From the inky black void before time, fine white mycelium stretched like bony fingers then coalesced into the mother of all. As she weaved the natural world, a second being followed her out of the void. On black wings he came like a shadow and in his wake, death. And so, the universe had balance. As the universe unfolded around them perfectly balanced, the two beings fell in love and from their coupling came humans. Creative and deadly. For a time, they worshipped Mother and Death. But as humans grew in number, they lost their respect for Mother and the fertile land she provided. And soon they were harming their home for profit. And while Mother grew distraught at this, Death was proud of the wars they fought, the ways they killed. So, when she decided to wipe the humans from the face of the earth, Death trapped her in a tree. Her only way out was the death of the tree. So, she sits year after year stewing in her anger over the abuse of the planet she created.

The tree sits, surrounded by overgrown fields with long grasses caressing it. An ever-present morning mist moistens its bark. Today, a man stands below its boughs, ax in hand. The mist thickens and tightens around him. Almost as if the earth itself waits with bated breath. He swings and the first thud reverberates up the trunk, his arms, and across the empty fields. As he works, he begins to sweat. But he is strong and sure in his swings and within minutes the tree is leaning. With a loud crack it snaps from its stump and crashes to the ground. Its branches snapping and stabbing the soft earth. There is a second crack as the trunk splits open like the seam of an overfilled garment. Thick moist earthy rot fumes out of the crevice followed by hands with green tinged fingers that clamp down on the bark. Mother crawls out, a mane of mushrooms on her head. She inhales with a curled nose as the man stares at her wide eyed. she climbs from the tree and approaches the man. Mycelium stretch from her feet through the soil and into his. Slowly they feed her his nutrients as he remains rooted to the spot. Mother passes him and the mist envelopes her, washing her parched skin. She walks toward the nearest town, her steps light on the ground leaving mushrooms in her wake. The town sits ten miles away from the site of the tree. Mother encounters no one else on this misty morning and when she reaches the town it appears to still be sleeping. Fire blazes in Mothers' eyes as she looks at the town. A disgusting blight on her beautiful earth. A light breeze whispers down the street and an empty can rolls toward her ting tinging on the concrete. She raises her hands to the sky drawing thunder clouds overhead. Lightening pummels, the road until it is turned to rubble and the scorched earth shines through. The cacophony draws the townspeople from their beds and as the storm clears, they see mother. Fiercely angry, drenched in rain. They stay sheltered in their homes until the ground begins to shake the dwellings. The people run screaming from their houses into what was once the street as their homes crumble. Mother traps their feet to the dirt with mycelium and the fungal network feeds her their fear and pain as the mycelium moves up through their bodies. When it's done, the town stands staring at the sky with blank eyes, a single fungus sticking out of their open mouths. Mother slides down into the soil feeding the earth the stench of humanity and her righteous anger. The planet wakes to the feeling of tiny insects crawling on its surface and it reacts. Mother feels death's gaze upon her, the approval warming her skin. She did not want to please him, but she would have her vengeance. She travels through the soil so he cannot follow, certain he wants to trap her again. She crawls from the dirt hundreds of miles from the town she replaced with fungus. A white clapboard church stands before her, the lead paint chipping off. She feels the soil cringe away from the shedding specks. Boisterous singing comes from inside the building. Happiness spills from its seams and Mothers stomach churns. She strolls through the front doors bringing with her a chilly wind. The congregation turns to look, their voices faltering at the sight of her.

    She spits green phlegm on the floor and from it a plant grows. "I am the only god," she says. Nervous laughter greets her proclamation, and steam rises from her skin. She feels no love for these, her children. They belong to death. She sees him when she looks at them.

    The pastor steps into the aisle, the room so quiet you can hear a pin drop. He clears his throat. "You have no power here, demon," he says with a little shake in his voice.

    Mother laughs hysterically, the walls shaking with the sound. She strides to the pastor and connects her lips to his. He stumbles back and falls onto the floor. His lips are stained green from her kiss, and he places his hand upon his stomach as it starts to swell. Vines explode out of him sending blood and intestines across the church. The congregation screams and turns for the door, but the vines slam it shut.

    "Where the fuck is your god now?" Mother asks as the vines attack the church members. She walks out the front door, the screams of the dying ringing in her ears. She has plans for the earth. Big plans. As the screams in the church echo behind her, Mother lets the wind lift her. Light as a feather she drifts through the sky. Birds flock around her with cries for help. They lead her to a field not so unlike the one death had trapped her in. Several men are standing in the field with guns shooting birds. Mother lands behind the men on silent feet. With a nod she encourages the birds to stand up for themselves. The birds swarm the men cawing and pecking until the men lay still in the dirt, their blood watering the soil. Mother rises on wings of her own and leads the birds to town where they attack, ripping flesh from bones. She exalts in the sound of the humans dying. Now that the earth is waking, Mother can hear it screaming in pain. She follows the sound to a landfill. Rage makes her body quiver as she gazes at the heaps of trash. She strings trash together with vines until there is a giant hybrid monster made of trash and nature. It marches off towards the nearest populace. The rest of the refuse she tucks under the earth. Mother deeply regrets her love affair with death. She lets the feeling consume her as she calls forth storms to wipe major cities from the face of the earth. The effort makes her tired and she disappears into nature.

Death rides his pale horse across the earth in search of Mother. Nature runs rampant and the humans are all but gone. Trash monsters roam what's left of towns. When she first began her quest for vengeance, he enjoyed watching her work. Her creativity for death was remarkable, but if she killed all the humans, he would no longer have a purpose. As death rides, he feels his pale horse sinking into the earth. Death stands upon his steeds back as he sinks to his belly. He jumps from the pale horse's back and vines snatch him out of the air, pulling him tight to the ground. Death's body begins to sink into the earth in a bone crushing embrace. Soil covers his face and coats his mouth as he fights to break free.

From dust to dust, but not today. That is my mantra. For six hundred days I've neither washed nor pissed upon the earth. I try desperately to be more animal than human. It's the only way to live now. The maternal instinct of this world we called home is long gone. She's a gaping maw, ready to gobble up anything remotely human. The women said it's because we broke her heart. Because we'd poisoned her, and she'd had enough abuse. The men tried to reason with her. Gave her sacrifices. But there is no appeasing righteous anger.

From up ahead, I hear the shrill cry of a baby. I remember as a child watching the movie Tarzan, and I imagine I am him as I move on all fours through the forest. I stop just shy of the cry and watch as the baby is lowered from the trees to the ground. The second it touches the earth; the dirt sucks it inside. I shake my head at the stupidity of humans. Why should the mother be satisfied with the sacrifice of one so innocent? She thirsts for those above and she's Insatiable. Her hunger only gone when they are too.

As I turn to go, an arrow whizzes from the trees and imbeds in my calf. I allow myself a grunt of pain, but the damage is done. The ground sucks hungrily at my blood as I'm drug backward by the rope attached to the arrow. For almost two years I have managed to stay hidden from her. Now I'll never be welcome here again. The dirt has my scent, has tasted my blood. My camouflage is useless now.

As I am hoisted off the ground my fear of heights causes me to get dizzy and vomit. The earth swallows that too. I close my eyes until I feel myself stop. As I open my eyes, the shock is evident in theirs. I was not the animal they'd intended to catch.

Two years ago, I'd been just like them. Believing salvation lay in the trees. But the trees have turned against us too. They just don't know it yet. Perhaps it was a disease Mother gave to them to find us. And so, I've done my damnedest to become invisible to her. I cast off my humanity to become an animal.

They have questions I know, but they can't ask. Even the sound of a human voice Mother knows. They won't risk their safety for curiosity. They know they can't take me back to their village. My blood would tell the earth where to find them. The two men turn and leave me hanging upside down by my leg.

As my blood drips onto the soil below, I feel the tree quiver and begin to sink as the earth devours it to get to me. Each crack of the earth crushing the tree reverberates into my injured leg. I grab at the arrow and try to pull it from my leg. The shaft snaps and I plummet toward the earth throwing my arms out to slow my fall.

Landing hard on my back I roll quickly to my feet and hobble away. I can hear the ground opening behind me, but I don't turn. I only hope I'm fast enough. There is a creek up ahead and water is the last safe place on the earth. As I run, I feel my injured leg sink and I trip. With a tug, the ground slurps me back toward my captured foot and I claw at the ground with a primal scream that is silenced with a mouth full of dirt. From dust to dust, today.

I fall. Through darkness I fall for what could be eternity and I land hard. Pain blooms across my body and I groan. All the rules I've lived by the last two years mean nothing now that I've been swallowed by the earth. The belly of the beast is warm and for the first time in a long time, I lay still and just am. My body begins to tremble, and I wish I could say it wasn't fear, but the truth is, I am afraid. And I've lived in fear since the day the earth revolted against humanity. Above ground, I'd learned what to expect. Down here I know nothing. The darkness is all encompassing, and I find I miss the moon's glow. Colored spots dance in my vision as my eyes try to see light in the pitch dark. The air is moist upon my skin, and I roll to my knees. Stretching with my hands I try to find a wall to follow. They come in contact with nothing. My mind tries to conjure up monsters in the dark and my shaking intensifies. I stay on my knees until it passes. Without light, I don't know how much time passes before I stand. My breath crashes in my ears. Have I always breathed this loud? It wasn't so apparent above the ground where nature has its own sounds. I make every effort to slow my breathing. To make it less loud. Perhaps Mother has forgotten those of us she has swallowed. I hope with everything I am that she has at least forgotten me. Slowly and silently, I count backwards from five then slide my foot forward with my hands out. With each step, I feel blood slide down my leg and pain reminds me I am alive. That this is not the afterlife.

As I move through the darkness, I hear things scurry behind me. My mind whirls, filling with monsters. Mothers' creatures. I watched as her natural trash monsters ravaged my city. The thought of the unknown gives me shivers again. Breathing comes from behind me and the shivers get worse. My injured leg is dragging and slowing me down. I have the feeling that whatever is behind me is following the smell of my blood. I try to move faster, and my hands drop to my sides to keep me balanced. The breathing of the unknown creature and the scrape of my injured leg urge me to move faster. Sweat pooling under my armpits for the first time in two years. I'm afraid Mother will smell me now, but I can't stop the fear causing me to exert myself. Whatever is behind me is getting closer. I can feel its breath on my neck. My skin prickles with the sensation and I freeze. My heart is pumping so fast that my pulse is white noise in my ears and for a moment I can no longer hear the breath behind me. I stop breathing and wait. Something bumps into me and bioluminescence flares.

    I cringe away, the sudden light hurting my eyes. My blood runs cold as I squint at my pursuer. Leaves twine through a mostly decayed human corpse. The sound I thought was breathing appears to be air rustling dead leaves as the creature moves. There is no water here to feed the plant life holding the creature together and it snaps its teeth at me. I feel a sudden pain in my open wound and look down. A vine from the creature is sticking through my leg. Upon contact with my blood, the dry leaves seem to perk up. Quickly I yank the vine from my leg and try to run.

    The undead creature chases after me, its bioluminescence glowing brighter. Tendrils of the plant crawl after me and I'm forced to watch my steps as I run. One snakes around my ankle, and I trip sprawling face first on the ground. The creature twines around me and I begin to rip at the foliage with my hands and teeth. Green juice spills down my chin and stains my hands. I claw and I shred until the plant is in pieces. Without the vine to support it, the body crumbles into bones at my feet.

    Slowly I slide away from the bones and keep a wary eye on them as the bioluminescence fades to a dim glow. The stain on my hands and face glow faintly as well and I hold my hands out to light my way as I return to my feet. I need rest but I am afraid to stay near the remnants of the creature. As I struggle on, I am once more surrounded by the complete dark of the belly of the beast. Not for the first time in the last two years, I ache for another human. Someone to reach out and touch. I long for a hand to hold, but I fear I am all that is left of humanity except the two men in the tree who shot me. Being alone had always comforted me in my old life. Now it is a curse and I struggle with the impulse to lay down and let Mother have me, for what is there to live for? But I continue to walk. I walk so long my leg heals. My stomach growls and echoes through the inside of the earth making it more monstrous. My tongue is thick with thirst and my head feels light. It is now I decide to lay down. To let Mother take me, but up ahead I think I see light. It is a force of will to keep my legs moving toward that. In the back of my mind, I know it is foolish. To think there would be light that bright in the bowel of the Mother, and if there was that it would even be safe. But that longing for touch rears its ugly head again and I am certain that light means humans. And as much as my body is starved for food, my mind is starved for connection. Two years, I have been silent as an animal. My safety above all else, but on the cusp of death, reason flees me. I struggle to put one foot in front of the other as my weakened body begs me to sit down, to give it rest. The light blinds me now after so long in the dark. My knees sag and I let gravity take me with a promise to myself to only rest for a minute, but my eyes droop.

When my eyes flutter open, I am once again blinded by light and at first, I think it's the sun. How I've missed him, a reminder that I am still alive. After a few blinks I realize the bright light is coming from a fire. Fear cramps my gut and I try to flee. Strong arms hold me down and shushing fills my ears as I try to flail.

"You're safe. You're safe."

I want to believe those words, I do. But fire means exposing myself to Mother more than I already have. My struggle tires me, and I slowly relax because my body can't keep going.

"You're very fortunate to have found us." A man's face hovers over mine, his mouth stained green. He smiles with green teeth. I feel hands release me and I slowly sit up with his help.

"I'm Jerimiah. Welcome to Bliss. What's your name?"

"I . . . I'm Harper." My voice sounds strange to my ears. I haven't used it in two years. The sound of my name is even stranger. I don't recognize myself as her any longer.

"It's nice to meet you Harper," he says as he hands me a cup of green liquid.

My nose crinkles as I sniff the liquid. It smells like the forest just after it rains. The smell of it makes me forget for a moment nature is no longer safe. Call it nostalgia for the forest before Mother became angry. Tears smart my eyes and I don't bother to wipe them away.

"Hey," Jerimiah says as he places his hand on my arm. "We've all been there. But I promise you're safe."

"Safety is an illusion," I say. Memories surge of my time in the tree. My colony thought we were safe. That we had tricked Mother, but she always finds us humans.

Jerimiah wraps his hand around mine on the cup. "Everything that happened above was to get us below. Here in Bliss, Mother takes care of us." His hand urges the cup toward my mouth and I'm too exhausted to fight.

My body hasn't had sustenance in who knows how long. The liquid touches my slips and slides down my throat. Bliss wraps around me and I feel safe. The feeling is foreign to me, and I relax into it like a nice hug. Drowsiness weighs down my eyes and I sink back and stare at the ceiling. Jerimiah feeds me more of the green juice until I fall asleep. Every time I wake, he feeds me more green juice. Time passes, but I don't know how much. When I first woke, he said us, but he is the only one I have seen so far. When I'm awake I hear other people. Jeremiah tells me these people have been saved by Mother. That they drink from her and the green juice he feeds me is her nectar. The thought that Mother now sustains me after I spent years fearing her churns my stomach. But the nectar is making me stronger. Jeremiah has offered to show me Bliss today, so like a good girl I drink the nectar he brings me. Being here, drinking the nectar has made me feel safer than I have in years. I am eternally thankful to Jeremiah and whoever these people are for taking me in because I never thought I'd feel this way again. Especially as the earth swallowed me. Jeremiah says the earth saved me because she knew I was hurting. With each sip of nectar, I start to believe him. I'm feeling better than I have in years. Jeremiah takes my arm and helps me stand and I realize I have been on a ledge this entire time. A set of narrow stairs lead down to my right, below us is Bliss. People are gathered below us talking and laughing and drinking nectar. Encircling them in the large, cavernous room is a natural stone basin full of nectar. Above the basin are tree roots sticking through the ceiling of the cavern. The nectar drips from the roots and keeps the basin full. I turn and behind me is a dark tunnel and I presume this is where I came from. The dark looms at me and I sway. Jeremiah's grip tightens and I smile at him as he keeps me upright.

"Come, meet the others," he says and tugs me Towards the stairs.

His hand remains on my arm as we descend into Bliss. Jeremiah introduces me to the gathered crowd and their names and faces blur together as my head swims from the interaction. They welcome me with open arms, and we laugh and dance and fuck around the giant bonfire under the earth. We paint each other's bodies with nectar, until our skin is dyed green. This goes on for hours, days, weeks, or more. Time is irrelevant when you're safe. The feeling oozes from my skin and mixes with the nectar before it is licked from my skin. Living like this, I can't believe I ever feared my Mother. To think she could turn on me and wish death. More people are brought in and they're vaguely familiar. I rub at my leg where I was shot with an arrow, and it clicks. These are the men who shot me, but there are no hard feelings, only bliss. At some point we calm, and we sleep in a pile of green tinted bodies. And I dream of babies crying and the earth swallowing them. When I wake and crawl from the pile, everyone else is still asleep and I realize there are no children here. No pregnant women despite all the sex. My hand trembles with a cup of nectar in it and it sloshes onto the ground. No more children.

Silently I climb the stairs back to the tunnel because I remember the old way of living and this is not life, only Bliss. And even if outside that cavern I am not safe, I feel alive. Invincibility still fills my veins because the nectar has not worn off, and I feel safe as I enter the black tunnel. My body glows from the nectar on my skin and it lights my way. I have to make it back to the surface, to the water, the only truly safe place left on earth. Silence wraps around me as I move through the tunnel, back the way I came who knows how long ago. This time I do not encounter a skeleton animated by vines, but I do end up in another cavern. There is a man hanging on the wall wrapped in vines. His eyes are closed, and his chest rises and falls with breath. I begin to pull and rip at the vines until they loosen, and he falls into my arms. His face is pale, a stark contrast to his black clothing. I laid him down and smooth dark hair off his forehead. His eyes flutter open.

"You hurt?" I ask as he sits up.

"She can't hurt me, I am death."

If Mother earth exists, I suppose I shouldn't question if death does. "Then could you, I don't know, kill her?"

He laughs, the sound ricocheting around us. "Why would I do that?"

"Because she is murdering humans. Because she trapped you."

"The trapping was tit for tat. As for you humans, you're stupid as a whole and she's got a point killing you."

"When you're done ferrying our souls, then what will you do?" I ask.

He laughs again. "I don't ferry souls. I am here for balance. I've simply enjoyed watching you humans kill each other. You get more creative as the years go by."

I cross my arms and glare at him. "Then can you at least put me back above ground so I can go to the one safe place left on earth?"

"The safest place is right back there drinking your nectar and going mad."

"That's not living," I say. "Please just show me how to get out of here. I want to see the sun."

Death snaps his fingers, and we are standing in the forest a pale horse running at us. A soft breeze clacks the bare branches together and I breathe fresh air. Life fills my lungs and I exhale a sigh of relief. It's been so long since I had to live in fear that it takes me a moment before I lower to all fours.

Death laughs at me as he mounts his pale horse. "Get up here."

I climb up behind him. "I thought you didn't care about humans!"

"I don't. I enjoy death, and yours is impending. Where to Harper?"

"The ocean."

"That's your safe place?" Death laughs again. "Okay."

He nudges the pale horse, and it moves forward. It's been so long since I have seen animals as pleasurable companions. Now they are deadly or food. There is no in between anymore. As we ride, I see more of the animated corpses. They climb trees and I know they are pursuing the living. Ashamed, I look away, there is nothing I can do for them. My survival is all that matters.

Death weaves around towns infested with trash monsters and birds follow in our wake. They don't dare attack Death himself, but their eyes are on me. Fear nestles in my gut once more and it makes me feel sick. Any minute, Death's protection of me could slip. He doesn't care about my life. Only my death. To my surprise I eventually see the sea on the horizon. My stomach finally unclenches, and I realize I am hungry. Hungrier than I have ever been in my life. We've been travelling for days. In answer to my growling stomach, the birds that have been following us drop from the sky, dead at our feet. Death stops his pale horse, and we dismount.

"I'm sure this is your last meal human. Eat up," he says.

Too scared to light a fire now that I am once more on the surface, I eat the birds raw, my eyes furtively glancing about. While I gnaw on the birds, I spy a boat rocking against the shore. When my stomach is full, I walk toward the vessel. Death follows in my wake. There don't appear to be any holes in the hull, and we climb aboard. Death pushes us away from shore and with a small amount of regret I watch land disappear as I realize I didn't plan this out at all. I didn't even make sure I would be able to feed myself out here. Death smirks at me now that we're surrounded by water.

"Now what?" he asks as he leans against the rail and crosses his arms and ankles.

I shrug as the sun sinks below the horizon. Water laps against the hull and stars twinkle above. I lay down on the deck and stare at them. I'm alive and I've achieved my goal. What more is there? I hear something wet splash on the deck and sit up quickly. Nothing looks out of place, and I chock it up to being tense and lay back down. The sound comes again, and I jump to my feet. It comes from behind me, and I whirl. There is only darkness, and the sound comes from behind me again. I spin and a wall of black rises in front of me. It bubbles and squirms towards me and I scream. The seething black liquid swarms me and I fall backward into something wet, and the liquid mass falls on top of me filling my nose and mouth. I taste oil and I try to spit it out, but more drowns me. As I struggle to roll over and spit, more liquid pummels my back, bounces off the deck under me and into my face.

I hear Death's voice. "I told you it was imminent."

Black tears fill my eyes as I continue to drown, and he does nothing but watch. I was wrong, the water is as unsafe as land. In the end Mother will get us all.

Death watches Harper struggle for breath as the oil wraps around her face and fills her throat. There's a small smirk on his lips as he leans against the rail with his arms and ankles crossed. Mother's creativity thrills him.

When Harper goes still on the deck, the oil monster slides over the side and plops back into the water. The movement of it not unlike an octopus. Death moves to Harper's side and rolls her onto her back. Her lifeless eyes stare up at him. He bites his lip hard enough to draw blood then uses his finger to smear it on her lips.

She rolls over and vomits oil onto the deck before drawing a shaky breath. "You . . . you bastard."

"How about thank you? I could have left you dead you know."

"Why didn't you?"

"I've got plans for you."

Harper glares at him and he smiles. His plans involve her death yet again, but he decides it's best not to tell her. They have a long journey ahead of them.

"Come along human, we need a disguise."

"A disguise?"

"Me and you are both wanted by Mother."

"Then we're already dead."

"Such negativity. Where's your hope" he asks.

"It died on the sea with me."

Death laughs and takes her hand.

I yank my hand away from Death and find myself back in the community below the earth. The group of humans are fucking and painting each other green, and I glance at Death. He ignores the Bliss orgy and heads for the nectar pool and begins to paint himself. I follow him to the pool.

"Drink it," he says.

I scoop some into my hands and watch him out of the corner of my eye. Death does not drink the nectar. I turn away and swish it in my mouth, so it stains my teeth a fresh green then I spit it out and rub it on my skin. When we're done, he holds his hand out to me and I take it. The nectar pool is replaced by a crumbled town. An eerie wind rustles dried leaves and partially decomposed corpses stand with silent screams turned toward the sky. Blackened fungus creeps out of decaying flesh. I shiver because I know as bad as the rest of the world has had it, this town had it worse.

"This is where it started," Death says.

He leads me to a tree that is split in half and laying in a field. Death climbs inside and motions me to follow. I stand there staring. I do not trust Death. He watched me

THE WICKED ARE NOT ALLOWED IN THE GARDEN 55

die with a smile on his face and I know he has plans for me. My body turns away from the tree and I stare out across the field. A body stands there facing the tree, fungus coming from its face. Perhaps Death can stop her reign of terror. It is with that small smidgen of hope I turn back and climb into the tree. The inside of the tree smells horrible of earthy rot and feels oppressive, like a heavy weight is crushing and pulling me. There are tiny pinpricks of light, the deeper I push, and I fall towards them. My body begins to spin, the lights swirling around me, faster and faster until my body begins to tear apart at the seams. A scream eviscerates my throat as I am undone and burst into pieces. When I come to rest among the stars Death snaps his fingers and I reassemble.

"My god, that was spectacularly entertaining," Death says. "Had you drunk the nectar, that would not have happened."

"I don't want to be blissed out." I don't add that I didn't trust his reasoning for drinking it. "Where are we?" Darkness reaches towards us with clawed fingers and Death breathes deeply of it, then sighs contentedly.

"Home," he says. "The beginning."

"Why?"

"That tree we came through is the very tree I trapped Mother in. And all she had to do was come through the portal and she would have been home."

"What's that got to do with me?"

"You should have left me tied to the wall," Death says before he kicks me into the void.

My Arms and legs flail as the darkness opens to consume me. There is nothing for me to grab onto and stop my momentum as the darkness slurps me inside. I become lost in it. My body stretching like taffy as the void remakes me. Once done, it shows me a reflection of myself. One eye is now milky white, the other coal black. My hair falls out and floats around me. Anger crashes over me sweeping me out of the void to the waiting Death.

"What the fuck did you do to me?" I ask as lightening cracks between the stars.

"I gave you power. You need never fear her again."

My fingers roam gingerly over my scalp, and I scream so violently it rips a tear in the fabric of the universe. More than anything Mother did or could do, this stings. I am no longer me. No longer human. Now what do I care for human problems. "Why?" I ask him.

"To stop her."

The lies rolling off his tongue are pretty, and God I'd like to believe them, but he did not do this to stop her. I am not so naïve as to think that. With no idea what I am, or how to live this way, there is no recourse but to follow him back to earth. We emerge from the tree, the decomposed fungal person still standing guard. The breeze feels different, welcome. It caresses my skin like a pet begging for attention and I let it soothe my frayed mind. I close my eyes as the breeze washes over my bald scalp. As the wind plays with me, I open my eyes to find Death staring at me with a smirk and I realize I hate him.

    Death leads me, I'm afraid like a lamb to a slaughter. I don't yet understand this new body and its capabilities. Nor why he suddenly wants to stop Mother or what he thinks I can do to her. And I'm no longer positive I want to. She was honest in her pursuit of human death. He wants something more. Something I can't quite put my finger on, and I don't like it. We're trapped in a game I don't yet know the rules to, and he'd better hope I never find out.

    Death whistles and the pale horse appears. We climb on his back, and he conveys us across the earth. I watch the scenery pass with disinterest as my mind whirls with what's coming. What could Death be planning? The pale horse carries us into a section of forest that is thicker than the rest of the surrounding land. The horse takes us into a clearing and stops. I dismount and look around. Something solid slams into the back of my head and I crash to the ground dazed. Death flips me over and I see he is holding his scythe. He rakes it down my stomach and blood gushes out as I scream in pain. Death ties my hands above my head with vines then lashes my feet together. I shake my head to clear the stars still swirling in my mind, but he places his hands in the wound and pulls my flesh apart. Death disappears into the trees, and I crane my head to look around. Lightening crashes all around me as I struggle to get free. I realize it is in response to my emotions, and I try to calm so I don't inadvertently strike myself. Blood rolls down my sides and pools under me on the ground and I wait for the earth to swallow me again. Before that happens, I see Mother herself walk out of the trees. The foliage parts for her and she approaches me with a confused look on her face, kneels at my side and looks down into my discolored eyes. As she looks at me, I hear a thud, and she slumps over my prone form. Death stands behind her with a large rock in his hands. He tosses the rock down and grabs her by the shoulders then shoves her head into the gash in my stomach. I scream again as he continues to cram her body inside mine. My stomach swells and I feel like I'm going to vomit. After he crams her feet inside me, he sews my stomach shut. I feel Mother stretch inside my body, and I scream again as we start to absorb each other. Death takes my bound feet and drags me to a large stone coffin that is set in the earth.

    "You should have left me tied to the wall," he says as he lowers the lid on the coffin.

    Darkness smothers me and my insides burn like fire. Mother fights to control my body and I fight right back. Our anger fuses as our bodies become one. Our memories intertwine and I no longer hate her. She seems justified. Now that I am no longer human, she does not hate me. Now our hate is combined for Death himself. I know he counted on our hate for each other to keep us stuck in this box fighting, but I remember

THE WICKED ARE NOT ALLOWED IN THE GARDEN 57

the portal in the tree he made for Mother, and I search with my senses for the portal in this coffin. It lays in the corner by our right foot, and we shimmy into it. We're ejected into space next to the void and I notice the tear my scream made in the fabric of the universe. Mother and I move toward the rip. We slide through it into a universe where Mother never bore Death's children. Where she plucked her own seed from her scalp, and they populated her perfect earth. Below us they exist on a lush vegetative planet she controls. I can feel Mother's yearning for it. It's untainted by Death's desires. We descend and walk among the foliage. Through her, I see the beauty in nature once more. Tall thin creatures emerge from inside trees and follow us. Their eyes watch us hungrily. Mushrooms grow along our skin and the watchers turn away. Small creatures emerge from furrows in the ground and skitter around our feet. Mother is at peace in this perfect world. I can feel she wants to stay. I urge her to bring the creatures home with us. Death must pay. We build mycelium stairs to the stars and the creatures follow us up and through the tear to our universe. Back through the portal we enter our stone coffin. Mother takes over our body and roots shoot out our sides busting through the stone into the earth. They stretch far and wide connecting to the forest around us. Death has left the forest. I call down the lightening and it breaks up the dirt above our coffin. We explode from our grave, roots holding us above the ground. Lightening cracks around us and rain drips from the sky. Mother's children from the other universe funnel out of the portal behind us into the forest and scatter. My white eye shows us the dead walking the earth because of Mother's hate. We feel nothing at the sight. I have shed my humanity.

Death walks the earth, his fingers caressing leaves. They turn black at his touch, curling up and snapping off. He is free of Mother once and for all. Trapped inside a body that hates her, she will never be free. At war with herself for eternity. The laughter of children echoes behind him, and he whirls. Death knows for a fact all of the children are dead. Every death he feels like an orgasm that ripples through his body making him purr with ecstasy. There is nothing behind him but forest and uneasily he begins his walk again. The forest seems to grow thicker around him making him claustrophobic. He walks with his hands out killing any shrubbery that dares touch him. Death passes through an overgrown graveyard and calls the dead forth from their graves with a whistle. Skeletons claw their way up from the dirt and follow in his wake. All of this green life makes him uncomfortable. Reminds him of the being he should have loved, but Death is incapable of the feeling. The dead give him peace. Long limbed pale creatures climb from the trees around him whispering his name. Warily he moves away from them at a quicker pace. The skeletons forming a border around him as he moves. Little creatures spring from the ground and attack the skeletons. Death begins to run. He runs so far and so fast that he leaves the forest and enters a rundown city. Death hides inside a crumbling building. He's unsure how Mother can still hold so much power over the land locked in her coffin, but Harper must not be as strong as he gave her credit for. A storm brews overhead and green creeps across the floor and walls of the building moving closer to Death until he is backed into a corner. Lightning strikes the building, and it catches on fire. Death rushes into the street, the fire spreading across the city quickly. A wall of fire moves toward him. He runs back toward the forest to avoid the flames, but the forest thickens and moves toward him. Death finds himself trapped between a wall of fire and thick forest, both of them an impenetrable wall. He stands between them and notices the stone coffin sitting ten paces away. He's unsure how she got out, but he runs towards it, certain it's his only means of escape. Death crawls into the coffin and tries to use the portal. It isn't there. Before he can turn and leap from the coffin, the lid slams closed above him. Flames seal the stone coffin then plants wrap it tight. The earth opens and the coffin is swallowed by dirt. Mother and Harper, walk over the burial and spit on it.

"You should have left me dead," Harper says.

Nausea wracks our gut as we walk away from Death's grave. We fall to our knees and begin to vomit. I feel Mother leave me as fine white tendrils come out of my mouth and fuse together. As I vomit, more grows until Mother is standing before me. She leaves me there on my knees and disappears back into the foliage. From below the ground I hear Death screaming for us to let him out. And I believe that is justice.

Did you love *The Wicked are not Allowed in the Garden*? Then you should read *Rise of the Universal Army*[1] by Eady H!

[2]

Returning from the future, Emily's life is once more thrown into chaos, disrupting her quest to be reinstated. It's out with Creation Enforcement and in with the Universal Army. If it's not aliens, it's obscure government organizations and jealous exe's. Everyone wants a piece of her and there's not much to go around until she's cloned. Pissed about her abused DNA she does her best to reign in the Butcher before the universe runs with red.

Read more at eadyh.com.

---

1. https://books2read.com/u/booKvZ

2. https://books2read.com/u/booKvZ

Also by Eady H

Batshit musicals
Wacky John
Attack of the Pulpits

Double Creature Feature
Double Creature Feature

Valoryn Universe
The End of Creation Enforcement
Rise of the Universal Army

Standalone
Where the Dark Things Are
Two-Bit Detective
Broken Girl Broken World
The Wicked are not Allowed in the Garden

Watch for more at eadyh.com.

About the Author

Eady H is a cancer survivor who lives in Indiana with her twins. If she's not writing comedy horror she's writing herself in other universes. She loves all things weird and absurd and she's here to entertain.

Read more at eadyh.com.

www.ingramcontent.com/pod-product-compliance
Ingram Content Group UK Ltd.
Pitfield, Milton Keynes, MK11 3LW, UK
UKHW041842141224
452457UK00012B/586